HELLO, I'M THEA!

I'm *Geronimo Stilton*'s sister. As I'm sure you know from my brother's bestselling novels, I'm a special correspondent for *The Rodent's Gazette*, Mouse Island's most famouse newspaper. Unlike my 'fraidy mouse brother, I absolutely adore traveling, having adventures, and meeting rodents from all around the world!

The adventure I want to tell you about begins at Mouseford Academy, the school I went to when I was a young mouseling. I had such a great experience there as a student that I came back to teach a journalism class.

When I returned as a grown mouse, I met five really special students: Colette, Nicky, Pamela, Paulina, and Violet. You could hardly imagine five more different mouselings, but they became great friends right away. And they liked me so much that they decided to name their group after me: the Thea Sisters! I was so touched by that, I decided to write about their adventures. So turn the page to read a fabumouse adventure about the

THEA SISTERS!

Name: Nicky

Nickname: Nic

Home: Australia

Secret ambition: Wants to be an ecologist.

Loves: Open spaces and nature.

Strengths: She is always in a good mood, as long as she's outdoors!

Weaknesses: She can't sit still!

Secret: Nicky is claustrophobic — she can't stand being in small, tight places.

Nicky

COLETTE

Name: Colette

Nickname: It's Colette, please. (She can't stand nicknames.)

Home: France

Secret ambition: Colette is very particular about her appearance. She wants to be a fashion writer.

Loves: The color pink.

Strengths: She's energetic and full of great ideas.

Weaknesses: She's always late!

Secret: To relax, there's nothing Colette likes more than a manicure and pedicure.

Colette

Name: Violet
Nickname: Vi
Home: China
Secret ambition: Wants to become a great violinist.
Loves: Books! She is a real intellectual, just like my brother, Geronimo.
Strengths: She's detail-oriented and always open to new things.
Weaknesses: She is a bit sensitive and can't stand being teased. And if she doesn't get enough sleep, she can be a real grouch!
Secret: She likes to unwind by listening to classical music and drinking green tea.

Violet

Name: Paulina

Nickname: Polly

Home: Peru

Secret ambition: Wants to be a scientist.

Loves: Traveling and meeting people from all over the world. She is also very close to her sister, Maria.

Strengths: Loves helping other rodents.

Weaknesses: She's shy and can be a bit clumsy.

Secret: She is a computer genius!

PAULINA

Name: Pamela
Nickname: Pam
Home: Tanzania

Secret ambition: Wants to become a sports journalist or a car mechanic.

Loves: Pizza, pizza, and more pizza! She'd eat pizza for breakfast if she could.

Strengths: She is a peacemaker. She can't stand arguments.

Weaknesses: She is very impulsive.

Secret: Give her a screwdriver and any mechanical problem will be solved!

Pamela

Geronimo Stilton

Thea Stilton
AND THE
LOST LETTERS

Scholastic Inc.

Copyright © 2014 by Edizioni Piemme S.p.A., Palazzo Mondadori, Via Mondadori 1, 20090 Segrate, Italy. International Rights © Atlantyca S.p.A. English translation © 2015 by Atlantyca S.p.A.

The publisher does not have any control over and does not assume any responsibility for author or third-party websites or their content.

Published by Scholastic Inc., 557 Broadway, New York, NY 10012. SCHOLASTIC and associated logos are trademarks and/or registered trademarks of Scholastic Inc.

Stilton is the name of a famous English cheese. It is a registered trademark of the Stilton Cheese Makers' Association. For more information, go to www. stiltoncheese.com.

This book is a work of fiction. Names, characters, places, and incidents are either the product of the author's imagination or are used fictitiously, and any resemblance to actual persons, living or dead, business establishments, events, or locales is entirely coincidental.

ISBN 978-0-545-65602-3

Text by Thea Stilton
Original title *Amore alla corte degli zar*
Cover by Giuseppe Facciotto (pencils) and Flavio Ferron (color)
Illustrations by Barbara Pellizzari and Chiara Balleello (pencils), Valeria Cairoli (base color), and Daniele Verzini (color)
Graphics by Elena Dal Maso

Special thanks to Beth Dunfey
Translated by Emily Clement
Interior design by Kay Petronio

12 11 10 9 8 7 6 5 4 3 2   15 16 17 18 19 20/0

Printed in the U.S.A.   40
First printing 2015

LOVE LETTERS

When I woke up that MORNING, there was a strange feeling in the air.

I didn't hear the **sound** of pawsteps on the sidewalk outside my building, or the rumble of city traffic. All I heard was the **HAPPY** laughter of mouselings in the park nearby.

Brrrriiinng!

As soon as I went to the window, I realized why: It was snowing! Flakes as light as grated Parmesan were falling from the sky. A thick, white coat of snow had covered the **city**! It must have been coming down all night.

I threw open the window to breathe in the CRISP air — and just barely managed to dodge a snowball tossed by a mouseling playing with his friends.

"Sorry!" the little mouse cried.

I grinned at him. The snow had put me in a **great** mood. I was sure it was going to be a *special* day!

I had just started making some hot chocolate when the phone rang. It was my **BROTHER**, Geronimo. He edits *The Rodent's Gazette*, the most famouse newspaper on Mouse Island, where I'm a special correspondent. He was calling to tell me the office was **CLOSED** because

Sorry!

SNOW had blocked the streets.

So I decided to spend my snow day cleaning out the **ATTIC**, which was overflowing with old things. I **STARTED** with a bunch of clothes stuffed into two large trunks. I found two *lovely* vintage hats. After a little cleaning, they'd look great with my new dress!

Then I tried on a few costumes from an old acting class. I looked absolutely ridiculous as Little Red Riding Mouse!

Finally, I came across a **box of toys** from when Gerry Berry and I were young mouselings. So many memories!

Under some **STUFFED ANiMALS,** I discovered a few books from my days at Mouseford Academy. As I **leafed** through my favorite

So many memories!

textbook, a THIN bundle of envelopes fell from the pages. It was tied together with pink ribbon.

I didn't remember the **LETTERS**, so I OPENED ONE ...

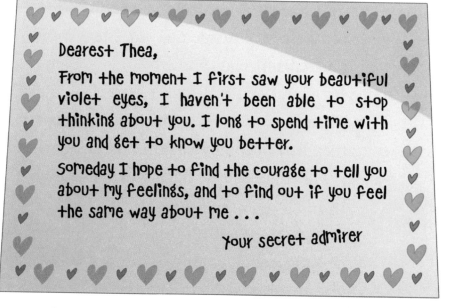

Dearest Thea,

From the moment I first saw your beautiful violet eyes, I haven't been able to stop thinking about you. I long to spend time with you and get to know you better.

Someday I hope to find the courage to tell you about my feelings, and to find out if you feel the same way about me ...

Your secret admirer

I remembered the thrill I'd felt so many years ago when I first found that LETTER on my desk! I'd received others, too, but I had never discovered who my mysterious ADMIRER was.

As I mulled over old memories, my cell phone LIT UP. It was a new email from my friends the THEA SISTERS! You see, a few years ago I'd returned to Mouseford Academy to teach a journalism class. Colette, Nicky, PAMELA, PAULINA, and **Violet** — the Thea Sisters — were my students, and they had become dear friends.

The mouselets had just returned from Russia, and they had a marvemouse adventure to tell me about! Coincidentally, their **STORY** also involved love letters.

I poured myself a cup of hot cheese and curled up on my couch to read . . .

MEETING
ON THE ICE

It was winter break at Mouseford Academy, and the Thea Sisters had just arrived in Saint Petersburg.* On their first afternoon there, they decided to go ice-skating at the rink in Palace Square.

While Colette, Nicky, Paulina, and Violet glided *smoothly* across the center of the ice, Pam couldn't tear her paws away from the railing around the edge. As soon as she dared to slide forward a step or two, she'd squeak, "Eek! I'm losing my BALANCE!"

Pam spun her paws in the air to keep from falling, but soon, her tail hit the cold, hard ice.

"Is everything okay?" a mouselet asked her, zooming over to give her a paw.

Pam scrambled up, **smiling**.

---

* Saint Petersburg is one of the biggest cities in Russia. Learn more on page 13.

"THANKS . . . My tail's a bit bruised, but there's no permanent damage. I'm such a klutz. I do better getting around on four *wheels* than on my own two PAWS!"

The mouselet giggled. "I get it! But skating isn't ʜᴀʀᴅ. You just need to bend your knees a little, keep your weight forward, and then let yourself *glide*."

It's not hard!

Pam tried out the mouselet's advice and moved forward a few **steps**.

"Slimy Swiss cheese! I can't believe I'm doing it! I'm really ice-skating!" she cried, beaming.

"Hey, Pam, are you getting private lessons over here?" Nicky joked, gliding over with the other THEA SISTERS.

Before Pam could reply, Colette's **EYES** widened. "B-but y-you're . . . Aleksandra Skettinova!" she spluttered.

The mouselet **motioned** for them to lower their squeaks. "Shhh! Yes, that's me, but no one knows I'm here. Anyway, I have to go practice, so, **BYE**!"

"Wait!" Colette tried to stop her, but the mouselet was already sliding over to the exit.

"Whoa, she's *faster* than a gerbil on a wheel!" Pam commented. "Who is she?"

"Aleksandra Skettinova is one of the best ice skaters in Russia," Colette explained. "She'll probably win the *figure-skating championship* we're going to in a few days."

You see, Colette had convinced her friends to spend their **winter** break in Russia so she could watch her favorite sport's championship in the fur.

"Frozen feta, how cool is that?!" Pam cried. "But now I'm a little tired from all this exercise. What do you say we find a snack?"

As the mouselets left the rink, a stack of flyers drew Nicky's attention. "Colette, look!"

Friday, Dec. 15th

GRAND CHAMPIONS' PRACTICE!

ICE PALACE
Saint Petersburg

Colette scanned the flyer. "Hey, that's THIS AFTERNOON! Mouselets, we absolutely have to go."

"But I wanted to visit the HERMITAGE* . . ." Violet moaned.

"Come on, Vi, the mouseum's not going anywhere. This is a ONCE-IN-A-MOUSETIME OPPORTUNITY!" Nicky said.

Oh, all right, Coco...

Violet was about to object, but then she saw the enthusiastic look on Colette's snout. "Oh, all right, Coco. Let's make like a cheese wheel and roll!"

* The Hermitage is a well-known museum in Saint Petersburg. Turn to page 65 to learn more.

Saint Petersburg

Saint Petersburg is one of the most significant cities in Russia, second in size only to the Russian capital, Moscow. It's located on the banks of the Neva River, which flows into the Gulf of Finland.

The city takes its name from Czar Peter the Great (1672–1725), who founded it in 1703. For two centuries, Saint Petersburg was the capital of the Russian Empire and home of the czars (rulers of Russia). In 1990, its historic district — which is full of palaces, monuments, and some of the most famous museums in the world — was declared a UNESCO World Heritage Site.

NEW FRIENDS, OLD RIVALS

Later that afternoon, the mouselets settled in the bleachers of the Ice Palace.

"This is actually pretty cool," said Violet. "We're snout-to-snout with champions!"

"Look, there's Aleksandra!" Colette cried, pointing to the center of the rink. A rodent in a matching costume circled next to her.

"There are individual and pairs events at this CHAMPIONSHIP. That must be Pavel Paponeci, Aleksandra's partner," Colette explained.

"Look how gracefully they move together!" Paulina said.

"They train together for at least three hours a day. That's how they create that perfect synchronicity of movement," said Colette.

"Check out those two over there. Their synchronicity is a little off," observed Violet, pointing to two SKATERS in RED.

The mouselet was ranting at her partner. "You messed up again! If this routine bombs, it'll be all your fault!"

Colette recognized the skater. "That's Katerina Rattotova. She's known for her triple axel* — and for her unpredictable personality."

Just then, Aleksandra stopped for a break. She glanced up at the bleachers and spotted the Thea Sisters waving their paws at her.

"Hey, you're the mouselets from this morning! Are you skating fans?" asked Aleksandra, gliding over to them.

"Yep, we're fans of skating — and of you!" Colette replied with a big smile.

---

* The *axel* is a spinning jump invented by the skater Axel Paulsen. It's considered the most difficult jump in figure skating.

The mouselet blushed. "Oh, THANK YOU."

Just then, Katerina slid over and STOPPED suddenly near them. "You're not worn out already, are you, Aleksandra?" she said nastily. "You and Pavel seem out of sync today. And let's not squeak about your RIPPED costume. Beating you will be easier than taking cheese from a mouseling! Ha, ha, ha!" She took off like a flash.

WORRIED, Aleksandra looked down at her costume. Colette reassured her, "It's just a torn ribbon. I can fix it myself if you'd like!"

She RUMMAGED in her purse and pulled out a small case with a needle and thread.

"You never know when you'll need to make a quick fix!" she explained to Aleksandra. A moment later, Colette had SEWN the ribbon back onto the costume. "Just like new."

"I don't know how to thank you," the SKATER said.

Colette grinned. "Watching you perform is thanks enough!"

Aleksandra skated off. But at the end of *practice,* she sped back over. "Mouselets, would you like to explore the city with me?"

"Sure, that sounds great!" Nicky cried.

Pavel **joined** the group. "Sandra, are these mouselets your friends?"

"THEY ARE NOW! Mouselets, this is Pavel. Pavel, this is . . ."

Violet stepped in. "We're Violet, Colette, Nicky, Pam, and Paulina . . ."

"But you can call us the THEA SISTERS!" Pam concluded.

It'll only take a second!

EXPERT ADVICE THAT'S TRÈS CHIC!

Aleksandra got changed and met her new friends *outside*. "Here I am, mouselets!"

Colette CLAPPED her paws. "I can't believe we're here in Saint Petersburg with a real, live skating champion. It's like a dream come true!"

Aleksandra smiled. "Aw, it's the least I can do to thank you for fixing my costume. Besides, I could use your expert advice."

"ADVICE?" Paulina exclaimed, looking surprised. "What kind of advice?"

"Advice on *style*," the mouselet replied. "You see, Countess Irina, the most famous NOBLEMOUSE in the city, is hosting a benefit party this evening, and she's invited all the skaters in the competition."

"Ah, now I get it," Colette said. "You need a **fancy dress**, right?"

Pam grinned. "Lucky for you, our Coco has a real passion for fashion."

"I can tell," replied Aleksandra. "And you can all come to the **party**, too, if you want!"

Colette was beaming.

"Of course we want to!"

Aleksandra led them down a wide boulevard lined with *luxurious* buildings. "We're on Nevsky Prospect, Saint Petersburg's main street," she explained.

For the next twenty **MINUTES**, the **mice** scampered along, oohing and aahing over the sights around them. Soon they reached a green building with graceful white columns.

"Oh, this place is famouse. It's the **Mariinsky Theater!**" said Violet. Her mother, an **opera singer**, had performed there many times.

"That's right!" Aleksandra nodded. "And right behind it is a place that should be famouse — my favorite *boutique*!"

The mouselets followed their new friend into a small store filled with **ELEGANT**

The Mariinsky Theater!

gowns. They called out compliments as Aleksandra tried on fancy dresses, and they even tried on a few new outfits themselves!

When it was time to say good-bye, Aleksandra said, "Mouselets, I have to go home and watch a video of my practice. But I'll see you tonight, right?"

"You got it!" Pam said.

How do I look?

With their paws full of packages, the Thea Sisters headed for their hotel, chattering about their afternoon of fun. And the best was still to come: That night they would attend the party at COUNTESS IRINA'S house!

PARTY WITH A PROBLEM

That evening, when the mouselets entered the countess's palace, their snouts fell open at the SPLENDOR around them.

"It's like a real castle!" Nicky cried.

An enormouse chandelier hung from the ceiling, its crystals clinking lightly in the breeze.

"Mouselets, are we dreaming?" Colette sighed.

Aleksandra's snout poked out of the crowd. "Welcome!" she cried. "I want to introduce you to the rodent of the house, the countess Irina. Come with me!"

The skater led them toward a small GROUP of mice. The Thea Sisters immediately recognized Aleksandra's rival,

Katerina. The elderly rodent of the house was **SQUEAKING** with the group.

"Countess, let me present my friends, the Thea Sisters," Aleksandra said.

"It's a pleasure," the **aristocratic** rodent replied. "To which noble house do these lovely young mouselets belong?"

"Oh, they don't belong to a NOBLE family," Aleksandra explained. "They are my friends, and —"

"Oh, poor dears, I'm so sorry for them!" the countess interrupted. "Without a noble family, what can a young mouse count on? Fortunately for me, I belong to a **family** of

ancient and distinguished lineage. We descend directly from the Romanovs!"

"As in Romanov pickles? Those are my favorite!" Pam said.

Violet gave Pam's tail a quick **TUG**. "Um, she doesn't mean the pickles, Pam. I think the countess is referring to the ancient family of **CZARS**!"

Katerina snickered. "Seriously? You didn't know that the Romanovs were the most famouse rulers of Russia?! Aleksandra, only you could have such clueless and uncultured **friends**."

May I have this dance?

Nicky was about to retort when the **ORCHESTRA** struck up the first notes of a lively tune. Pavel and a few of his friends scurried over to them.

"Aleksandra, may I have this dance?" Pavel asked with a bow.

The mouselet *smiled*. "Of course!" Pavel's friends **introduced** themselves and asked the Thea Sisters to dance. A moment later, the six couples were spinning to the sound of the music.

Only Katerina was still without a partner, but she was soon distracted by the arrival of a rodent with an anxious look on his snout.

"Papa, you're late! The countess has been asking about you," Katerina scolded him. "Don't tell me you got held up at work again!"

"I did, unfortunately. I had to stay at the POLICE station to handle a very delicate case . . ."

"Blistering blue cheese!" blurted Katerina. "I know you're the best detective in the city, but it'd be nice if you could be on time for once."

"Well, I can't control the crime wave, my dear," her father said. "Last night there was a SERIOUS theft."

"What kind of theft?"

"Another piece from the **HERMITAGE MUSEUM** has disappeared. It's been months now, and we're still no closer to catching the thief. This time, the thief took a very precious ring. Look." He showed his daughter his cell phone. The screen displayed an ornate, jeweled ring.

"But . . . but that *ring* . . ." Katerina turned as pale as a slice of mozzarella. "I've seen it before!"

The ring is made with a rare gemstone called alexandrite. The stone was discovered in Russia in 1831, and it's named in honor of Czar Alexander II. The fine craftsmanship of the ring is typical of that time.

"Maybe you saw it when you visited the **MOUSEUM'S** Treasure Gallery," her father replied.

"No, that's not it. I saw it a few minutes ago — here, in this room!"

Her father **STARED** at her. "What are you squeaking, Katerina? That's not possible . . ."

"But I know I saw it!" replied his daughter. She scanned the room, and then pointed to a couple of dancers WALTZING across the ballroom floor. "There, SHE'S wearing it!"

SUSPiCiONS

The music ended, but the dancers remained in the center of the room, waiting for the **orchestra** to begin again.

Pavel was still holding Aleksandra's paw. He looked into her **EYES**. "We get along well both on and off the ice, don't we?"

Aleksandra **SMILED** up at him. Before she could reply, Katerina and her father interrupted the moment.

"There! She has it!" Katerina said, **POINTING** to Aleksandra.

"Miss, would you follow me, please?" the detective said.

Aleksandra was **surprised**. "Of course, but . . . what's going on?"

"I would prefer to squeak in PRIVATE. Come along."

34

Aleksandra shot a look of alarm at Pavel and the Thea Sisters, who followed her and the **detective** into the next room. There he asked Aleksandra to show him the ring she was wearing. **Without hesitation**, Aleksandra held out her paw.

"You see? It's identical!" Katerina insisted.

"It does MATCH," her father admitted, looking thoughtful.

"It matches what?" Pavel asked.

"The ring that disappeared from the Hermitage last night," the detective explained.

Aleksandra's tail twitched nervously. "But . . . but this is an old family heirloom. I've been wearing it for years! Before that, it belonged to my mother. I swear it on a stack of cheese slices!"

"This must be a *misunderstanding*," said Colette. The other mouselets nodded in agreement.

"That's possible, but for now I must take this ring to the station," replied Katerina's father, a serious look on his snout. "I'll have to open an investigation. Miss Aleksandra, where were you **last night** between eleven p.m. and one a.m.?"

"I . . . was at home, alone," Aleksandra said hesitantly. "I'm usually asleep by then, but I stayed up late watching videos of my **practice**."

"Then no one can confirm your story?"

"**NO**," the mouselet admitted.

"You're not **ACCUSING** her of stealing the ring, are you?" Pam burst out.

The detective **sighed**. "I'm not accusing her . . . for now. First, we must examine the ring to **VERIFY** it's the one that was stolen. Miss Aleksandra, I'll need you to **STAY HOME** for the next few days in case we need to call you in for questioning."

"But the **CHAMPIONSHIP** begins in a few days,"

the skater protested. "I have to train!"

"I'm afraid you'll have to miss your training. Sorry." The **DETECTIVE** stalked away.

Katerina shot a defiant look at her **rival**. Then she scurried after her father.

As soon as they were alone, the Thea Sisters surrounded their new friend. Her eyes were shining with tears. "My ring! How could the detective think it was **STOLEN** from the Hermitage?"

Colette put a paw on her shoulder. "Don't worry, Aleksandra! I know this is all a big misunderstanding."

Paulina nodded. "Let's see if we can *figure* it out. First of all, who gave you the ring?"

"My mother gave it to me when I turned eighteen," the mouselet **explained**. "It belonged to my great-great-grandmother, and it's been passed down from generation to generation. It's always been in my **family**."

"Then that'll be easy to prove," Violet said encouragingly. "Snout up, Aleksandra! In a day or two, this whole thing will be nothing but a **BAD MEMORY**."

"By then, it'll be too late," Aleksandra cried. "The **CHAMPIONSHIP** is in three days!" She sank into a chair and buried her snout in her paws.

There was a moment of **silence**. Then Pavel scurried over and took her paws in his. "Don't worry. I'll **help** you!"

"And so will we!" the THEA SISTERS joined in.

"Mouselets, do you remember what we learned from Thea in our **investigative** journalism class? Let's make a plan!" said Colette. She pulled a notebook out of her purse and began scribbling notes.

PLAN TO HELP ALEKSANDRA

* INVESTIGATE THE THEFT AT THE HERMITAGE: NICKY, PAULINA, VIOLET

* RESEARCH ALEKSANDRA'S RING: PAVEL, PAM, COLETTE

* CHEER UP THE BEST SKATER IN THE WORLD: EVERYONE!!!

THE CLUE IN
THE ALBUM

Early the next morning, Pavel, Colette, and Pam hurried over to Aleksandra's house.

"I have just the thing to cheer you up — a Russian breakfast!" Pavel cried, pulling an apron out of a kitchen cupboard. "Can someone give me a paw?"

Pam stepped forward at once. "If you're making treats, you can count on me. Especially if you need helping tasting 'em!"

The ratlet laughed. "Get ready to try a famous RUSSIAN delicacy: blini!"* He took out flour, eggs, yeast, milk, and butter and started to MIX everything together.

The result was a steaming plate of traditional Russian pancakes piled up high.

"They look whisker-licking-good,"

* Blini are very thin pancakes.

Pam exclaimed. "I'd like to eat them all!"

"Hold it right there!" the ratlet said, laughing. "Blini always bring a *smile* to Aleksandra's snout. We'll serve them with honey and marmalade."

They brought the blini to their friends,

who were curled up together on the couch.

"Wow, Pavel, those look tastier than toasted Brie!" exclaimed Aleksandra.

The ratlet smiled back shyly.

"What have you two been up to?" asked Pam, nodding to an old PHOTO album on Aleksandra's lap.

"We're trying to find a picture that proves the ring's been in Aleksandra's family for

Those look tasty!

Yum!

ages . . . Hey, look here!" Colette replied, pointing to a photo of a mouselet wearing a ring on her finger.

"It's small, but it looks like your ring, Aleksandra!" Pam said.

"Who is this mouselet?" Colette asked.

The skater examined the photo uncertainly. "I think that's my great-great-grandmother, but I'm not sure."

"Could you ask your mother?" Pavel suggested. "Maybe she knows more about the ring's history."

"Good idea!" the mouselet cried, scampering off to find her phone. "Hmm . . . it's only eight o'clock in the morning here, so it's a little late for her!"

"Aleksandra's mom is in **CANADA** for a conference. So Sandra needs to figure out the TIME DIFFERENCE," Pavel explained.

About ten minutes later, Aleksandra returned.

"She told me that the mouselet in the picture is **YULIA**, my great-great-grandmother," Aleksandra said. "She was a maid in the court of Czar Alexander II. Unfortunately, my mom doesn't know ***anything*** else about her. But she told me to stay **CaLm** — she's going to call the detective."

"So everything's fine, then!" Pam cheered.

"Not exactly . . ." Aleksandra said. "She won't be back here until the *finals* . . . and I may not be competing if we can't **solve** the case in time!"

SURPRISES FROM THE PAST

"We don't have much time," Colette said. "But you know the first rule we learned in our **INVESTIGATIVE** journalism class?"

"Yep! Don't give up at the first sign of TROUBLE," Pam replied.

Aleksandra smiled. "Okay! So what do we do?"

"Let's keep looking through the album. If we find a **PHOTO** that shows the ring clearly, we can use it as proof that it's always belonged to your family," Colette suggested.

The mouselets continued to study the photographs, which had yellowed with time. At first, nothing popped out, until . . .

"**WAIT!**" Aleksandra cried, stopping at a picture of Yulia. She pointed to a piece of furniture in the background. "This mirror looks familiar . . . My mom still has that dressing table."

"Where is it?" Pam asked, **LOOKING** around.

"It's a little wobbly, so we put it in the **ATTIC**," Aleksandra explained.

"Well, come on then, let's move those tails! There might be something in a drawer that proves the ring belongs to your family," Colette said. "Never give up on a lead! That's the second *rule* — "

"From your investigative journalism course!" said Aleksandra, smiling.

Up in the attic, the mouselets spent a few moments letting their eyes adjust to the dim light. Old ODDS AND ENDS were scattered around the big room.

"The mirror must be OVER THERE," said Aleksandra. "But I don't know if it'll be useful to us . . ."

Colette opened all the drawers in the dressing table, but all she found in them was dust.

Pavel examined the back of the mirror, but then he shook his snout. "Nothing back here but bugs."

"Let's forget this old furniture and go get a second helping of those delicious blini," suggested Pam.

"Just a sec. I have this feeling there's something more here . . ." Colette murmured, touching the **back** of the mirror.

CLACK!

Suddenly, a COMPARTMENT they hadn't seen before clicked open under the center drawer.

"A secret compartment!" Pavel cried.

"**CRISPY CHEDDAR!** What do you think it's for?" Pam asked, surprised.

Colette **REACHED** her paw into the drawer. Inside was a bundle of envelopes tied together with a PINK ribbon.

"Secret LETTERS!" Colette exclaimed. "This has got to be a clue that'll help solve the **MYSTERY!**"

DEAR YULIA . . .

The mice scurried back DOWN to the living room. Colette and Aleksandra sat on the couch with the LETTERS spread over their knees, and Pam and Pavel gathered around them.

"Check it out! These are old LOVE letters," Colette declared a moment later. "Now we're cooking with cheese!"

They're old love letters!

"Read them to us," Pam urged her.

Colette cleared her throat, picked up the first LETTER, and began reading.

Dear Yulia,

I can only imagine what you must be thinking: Why is this ratlet I met once at court writing to me as if we were old friends?

My boldness is surprising even to me, but I cannot escape my desire to know you better. I was showing my latest creations to the czarina when you came into the drawing room to serve tea. Your presence lit up the room. I found I could not take my eyes off you.

I hope that my words do not offend you: I am simply following my heart, which tells me to seek your friendship. If you could find it in your heart to reply, you would make me the happiest mouse this side of Moscow.

Respectfully,
Your Ivan

"How *romantic*!" Colette sighed. "But who is this Ivan?"

"I don't know. Maybe if we keep reading, we'll **FIGURE** it out!" Aleksandra replied.

Dear Yulia,

What a joy it was to receive your reply! I did not dare hope that you wished to know me, too!

You asked me about myself. You already know my work, and there is little else to say. Even though I am now part of the czar's court, at heart I am just a simple ratlet who enjoys nothing more than a horseback ride across the Russian plains.

I would like to take you on a ride along the Neva when the snow has melted and spring brings life back to the land. Do I hope for too much?

With friendship,
Your Ivan

Aleksandra *plucked* the next **letter** out of the pile. "I'll read the next one."

Colette scooted a little closer to her friend so she could read over her shoulder.

Dear Yulia,

These days the world has become a sad place. Saint Petersburg is colder than ever. I walk along its paths with an empty heart beating beneath my fur.

It seems I have offended you, my dear friend, with my bold invitation.

You are right: I dared too much.

But if you would forgive me and offer me your companionship once more, I promise to be a better friend.

With anxious hope,
Your Ivan

"Poor Ivan!" cried Pavel.

The mouselets GIGGLED behind their paws. They weren't the only ones mesmerized by the love problems of this ratlet from another century!

"Do you want to read the next one?" Aleksandra asked, handing him the letter.

Blushing redder than a cheese rind, Pavel cleared his throat and began to read.

Dearest Yulia,
The news that you were ill has made me sick with worry! All the same, you cannot imagine my relief to discover the true reason you had not responded to my letters.
The sunshine is still timid, but I think that an outing would cheer you. If you agree, I'll collect you in my carriage at the time of your choosing.

With great affection,
Your Ivan

"Pickled Parmesan pierogis, don't stop! All right, I'll read the next one so we can find out if Yulia and Ivan had their **date** or not," cried Pam, grabbing the last letter.

CLUE!

Sweet Yulia,

The hours that we spent together flew by like the wind across the Neva River. No mouselet is sweeter or wittier than you. Meeting you has put a sparkle in my dull days!

I am creating a piece of jewelry for the czarina that has kept me occupied for many hours, but as soon as I am free, I would love to spend more time in your company.

With all my love,
Your Ivan

"It's a shame that there aren't any other letters. We'll never know how it **ENDED**," Aleksandra sighed.

"Wait, wait, wait, wait," Colette said. "He wrote *jewelry* here . . . which means that Ivan was a jeweler! Are you thinking what I'm thinking?!"

"He could have made the ring Aleksandra inherited!" Pavel cried.

"Exactly. But why would there be an identical one at the Hermitage?" Colette wondered.

A LUCKY MEETING

While Colette and Pam were reading letters with Aleksandra and Pavel, Violet, Paulina, and Nicky had arrived at the Hermitage Museum.

"What a marvemouse *palace*!" Nicky commented, admiring the ornate facade.

"This is the Winter Palace, which was once home to

What a marvemouse palace!

the **CZARS**," Violet said. "It's just one of the buildings where the **MOUSEUM'S** collection is displayed."

"You've really read up on this, eh, Vi?" Paulina asked, smiling.

Violet blushed. "Yes, well, I've *dreamed* of visiting this mouseum for years. Of course, I never imagined I'd be here to investigate a *mystery*!"

Inside, all of the mouselets were struck squeakless. The Hermitage was enormouse! Their first stop was a long gallery with a richly **PAINTED** ceiling.

"Where do we start?" Nicky asked.

"Why don't we head for the room where they kept the **ring**? It should be this way . . . Come on, let's haul tail!" Violet said confidently.

Half an hour later, the Thea Sisters were still trailing through **corridors** and rooms filled with paintings, statues, drawings, and precious objects.

Violet turned a corner in hopes of finding the **Treasure Gallery**, but instead found herself snout-to-snout with an ancient sculpture. "I was sure the *jewelry* would be in this section . . ." she murmured. She was beginning to lose hope.

"You said the same thing *five minutes* ago," Paulina pointed out.

This isn't the Treasure Gallery!

"I know . . . I've read so much about this mouseum, I was sure I could find the RIGHT section. But now I'm lost like a rat in a maze!"

"Okay, **mouselets**, let's ask a guide for directions. I'll go find someone," offered Nicky, *turning* toward the nearest corridor.

By the time she realized that a rodent with his paws full of **BOOKS** was heading straight for her, it was too late: The pair smacked into each other, and books *FLEW* in every direction.

Sorry!

You shouldn't be running!

"Ouch!" the rodent cried.

Nicky blushed to the roots of her fur. "**Sorry!**" she said, giving the rodent a **PAW**.

"You shouldn't be running in the **MOUSEUM**," the mystery rodent said, scrambling to his paws.

Nicky realized that he wasn't much older than her. Behind his **GLASSES** was a pair of friendly, sparkling blue eyes.

"You're right. I was **LOOKING** for the Treasure Gallery, and . . ."

"Which **Treasure Gallery**?" the ratlet asked kindly.

"The one where the stolen ring was kept," replied Paulina, joining them. "Can you **help** us?"

The ratlet's snout clouded over for a moment. "Yes, I heard about the stolen ring. But you're heading in the **WRONG** direction."

"Um, I think that's my fault . . ." said Violet, blushing. "Could you tell us how to find the right room?"

"Sure, I'll take you there myself," the rodent replied.

"Oh, thank you!" Nicky said.

"It's no trouble at all. I'm going there, too. My name is Gavril, and I'm an art history student. I'm a research assistant for Professor Rattensky, who's studying the Romanov dynasty."

"We're Nicky, Violet, and Paulina," Nicky said. "Nice to meet you, Gavril. It's kind of you to help us."

"Oh, it's no cheese off my rind. Can I ask why you're so interested in that ring?"

The mouselets shared a look. They were all thinking the same thing: They could trust this kind RATLET.

The Hermitage Museum

Founded in 1764 by the empress Catherine II of Russia, the Hermitage Museum is located in the heart of Saint Petersburg. It's the most famous museum in the city, and one of the most well-known in all of Russia.

The museum is made up of five connected buildings. The most important is the Winter Palace, the ancient residence of the czars.

More than three million objects and works of art from all over the world are on display in the Hermitage: paintings, jewelry, sculpture, and much more! Among the major artists exhibited there are Leonardo da Vinci, Caravaggio, Titian, Paul Cézanne, Claude Monet, Vincent van Gogh, and Pablo Picasso.

THE TREASURE GALLERY

As they scampered along, Nicky began to **TELL** Gavril the story of Aleksandra and her family heirloom. "We're trying to **investigate** the theft so we can clear her name," she concluded.

Gavril **sighed**. "Well, mouselets, that job could be very difficult. For two months now, a thief has been stealing priceless objects from the mouseum. And the police don't have a **clue** who the culprit is!"

"Seriously?" Nicky said. "So the ring is only the most recent theft . . ."

Gavril nodded. "Several pieces of jewelry belonging to the Romanovs have disappeared like cheddar in a cheese grater. And they're all one-of-a-kind, *precious* pieces."

"If the police don't have any clues, it'll be hard for us to FIND any," Violet noted.

The little **GROUP** reached the Treasure Gallery. When they got their first glimpse of the amazing jewelry made of gold, crystal, and precious stones, the friends couldn't help letting out a sigh of admiration.

Professor!

"There's Professor Rattensky. I'll introduce you," Gavril exclaimed. "**PROFESSOR!**"

A tall rodent with glasses turned around. He had a thick **NOTEPAD** in his paw.

"Gavril, is that you? What's going on?"

"Professor, I'm back. I brought some rodents I'd like to introduce to you . . ."

"Back? You were gone?" the rodent asked in a confused squeak.

"Sometimes he can be spacier than an astrorat," Gavril whispered to the Thea Sisters. Then he replied, "Yes, I went down to the **archives** to check something, and on my way back I met these mouselets. They're investigating the theft of the ring."

The professor turned toward them. "Investigation? Are you with the police?"

Nicky smiled. "No, we're just trying to help a friend."

Professor Rattensky was silent for a moment. "Wouldn't you rather visit the MOUSEUM? If you like, Gavril could give you a *TOUR*. He's spent more time here than I have."

"Thank you, but first we must find out who stole the **ring**," Violet said politely but firmly.

"As you wish. Good luck, then!" Rattensky said. He turned back to the jewelry.

"We were hoping he could help us . . ." Nicky murmured.

"I'll help you," Gavril offered. "I know this mouseum like the back of my **paw**. Come on, let's go to my office."

A PHANTOM THIEF

Gavril took the mouselets to a room full of **filing cabinets**, photographs, and art history books.

"Welcome to my kingdom!" he joked. "This is where I spend hours and hours *STUDYING* the mouseum's collection. Luckily for me, the professor joined our staff two months ago, and he's a great expert on the last dynasties of the czars. We share this office, but he mostly stays in the galleries studying the *artwork*."

"Do you have any information on the ring and the other **stolen** objects?" Violet asked.

Gavril took a few documents out of a filing cabinet. "Here, this is everything."

"A **ruby** pin belonging to the Czarina Maria Aleksandrovna was stolen two months ago," Paulina read. "A SILK and *lace* fan from 1860 was stolen six weeks ago . . . A **pearl** bracelet belonging to the Grand Duchess Maria from 1865 disappeared five weeks ago . . ."

"Wait a minute . . . Can I take a peek at that LIST, Paulina?" Violet asked. She studied it for a minute. "These objects were all made during the reign of Czar Alexander II!"

"Just like the stolen ring!" Nicky exclaimed.

Gavril nodded. "EXACTLY. And that's just the tip of

Pin belonging to the Czarina Maria Aleksandrovna

Fan from 1860

Bracelet belonging to the Grand Duchess Maria

the cheese wedge. You see, the thief only steals jewelry from that period. And he always strikes on **Thursday nights**."

"Always on Thursdays? But why?" Nicky asked.

"**No one knows**," the ratlet replied. "Somehow he always manages to avoid the mouseum's security cameras."

"We need to *talk* to someone who knows everyone who comes and goes . . ." Violet murmured.

"You need **YURI**," Gavril said, nodding. "He's the head **security** guard. He'll be able to help us. Let's go!"

Gavril led the mouselets to a door down the hall and **KNOCKED**.

The door opened a crack, and a rodent with thick whiskers appeared.

"Gavril, it's you! And who are these

mouselets?" he asked.

"Yuri, let me introduce my new *friends*. They need to talk to the only rodent who knows everything that *happens* in this mouseum!"

Yuri laughed. "In that case, you're welcome to come in." He threw open the door.

"Whoa, that's impressive," Paulina exclaimed when she **SAW** the screens crowding the room.

"From here you can see every corner of the exhibit halls," the guard explained **PROUDLY**.

"Including the one the ring was stolen from?" Violet asked.

The rodent's snout grew serious. "Yes, but unfortunately that **THEFT** happened at night, when there was no one on duty. I left

the **SECURITY** cameras set to record, but the footage didn't show anyone entering the room."

"How is that possible?" Nicky asked.

Yuri shrugged. "I can't explain it. The thief must be a **PHANTOM**."

"Mouselets, we need a **plan**," Violet said. She turned to Yuri. "Are there regular visitors to the mouseum? The **THIEF** probably studied the exhibition room before he or she struck."

"Well, yes, there are many regular visitors," Yuri replied.

"Can you remember anyone who's visited a lot over the last two months?"

The rodent stroked his **whiskers** thoughtfully. "Well, a few come to mind. There's a **countess** who always looks swankier than soft cheese, an elegant **couple**

who only squeak French, and then there's a rodent always dressed in black with a white **flower** in his buttonhole, plus an *art* student who copies paintings. He likes to wear a funny SCARF with penguins on it."

Violet jotted down a few notes on her **notepad**.

"Now I must get back to work. I can't let any thefts happen on my watch! I hope I helped," said Yuri, guiding the group to the door.

"Let's go back to my office," Gavril suggested. "I can help identify a few of the SUSPECTS."

IDENTIFYING SUSPECTS

The mouselets returned to Gavril's office and gathered AROUND his desk.

"I know the countess Yuri mentioned," Gavril said. "I've been coming to the MOUSEUM for years, so I recognize a lot of the regular visitors."

"GREAT!" Violet cried. "Then we can make a list of potential thieves."

"The rodent who's always dressed elegantly is Countess Irina," Gavril **began**.

"**WE KNOW HER!** We were at her house for a party last night," Nicky said.

Violet nodded. "And now that I think of it, the countess had portraits of Alexander II and his family *hanging* from the walls of her drawing room . . ."

"Yes," Gavril **sighed**. "She's never been able to prove it, but she claims to be a descendant of the Romanovs. Collecting items that belonged to the czars is her *passion*."

"Then she could be the **THIEF**!" Nicky exclaimed.

Gavril slowly shook his snout. "But we don't have any proof! Plus there are the two French rodents, Antoine and Joséphine Duprés. They're the owners of a prestigious art gallery in Paris. They have a good **motive**, too! But the rodent dressed in black . . . I don't have any **IDEA** who he could be."

"It'll be hard to identify the student copying paintings, too," said Violet, who was taking **NOTES** on everything Gavril said.

The ratlet laughed. "Actually, he's the easiest of the bunch. That's Adrian, **my brother**."

Rodent dressed elegantly from snout to tail

Elegant French couple

COUNTESS IRINA

ANTOINE AND JOSÉPHINE DUPRÉS

????

Rodent with a white flower in his buttonhole

Art student with the penguin scarf

ADRIAN

"Your brother?" Violet said. "Are you sure?"

"Positive. I gave him that penguin scarf for his fourteenth birthday! It's his lucky charm."

"But why does he come to the mouseum every day?" Paulina asked.

"He's studying drawing, so I suggested that he copy the works on display," Gavril explained.

"It's a great way for an aspiring PAINTER to practice," agreed Violet. She shared Adrian's love of art.

Gavril smiled. "That's right. And what's more, my brother has an ironclad alibi . . . or perhaps I should say his alibi is made of marble!"

"Huh? What do you mean?" Nicky asked.

"Every Thursday, Adrian and I go to the

ADRIAN AND GAVRIL

CHESS CLUB in our neighborhood. We've been members since we were mouselings."

"Checkmate!" said Violet, smiling. "Okay, I'll take him off the list of suspects, then."

"We still have the others to think about: Countess Irina, the French couple, and the **MYSTERIOUS** rodent with the white flower," Nicky said.

Paulina grinned. "Sharpen your claws, **SISTERS**! It's time to see what we can dig up on our suspects."

THE INVESTIGATION CONTINUES

Nicky, Paulina, Violet, and Gavril scurried out of the office to begin the next stage of their *investigation*.

"We know where to find the countess, and the French couple is probably staying in a HOTEL," Violet said. "The rodent DRESSED in black, though . . . He's going to be harder to find than a cheddar chunk in a fancy cheese shop."

"Wait . . . didn't Yuri mention a white flower on his lapel?" said Nicky.

"Yes, why?"

"Look over there. I think we *found him*!"

Just a few yards away, a rodent matching the guard's description had thrown open the DOOR to the mouseum director's office.

"So it's final, then? You won't **sell** me Maria Aleksandrovna's treasure chest?" he said.

The mouselets could *hear* the director's squeak clearly from inside the office. "Not a chance. What belongs to the mouseum stays in the mouseum!"

The rodent's tail trembled with fury at this reply. **"You'll be sorry** you said that, or my name isn't Andrej Goudanov!"

He's over there!

You'll be sorry!

He slammed the door and **hurried away**.

"Andrej Goudanov!" Gavril exclaimed. "He's a famouse art collector. And rumor has it he'd sell his mother's last cheese rind to get his paws on new **relics**."

"Very suspicious," Nicky commented. "Why don't I *follow* him and see what I can find out?"

"You can't go alone," Gavril objected. **"I'LL COME WITH YOU."**

"We'll start tracking down the other suspects," Violet said. "Text us if you find out anything, and we'll do the same."

So the group split up. Gavril and Nicky scurried after Goudanov, and Paulina and Violet went to check out **luxury** hotels to see if they could *locate* Antoine and Joséphine Duprés.

They had no luck at the first two hotels.

But in the third, the receptionist RECOGNIZED the names of the two French collectors.

"Are they staying here?" Paulina asked HOPEFULLY.

"No, no." The receptionist shook her head. "They always have a suite *reserved*, but they're not here right now."

I know them. But they're not here . . .

"When was their last visit?" Violet asked. "Sorry to bother you — my, um, cousin has a *ring* she's hoping to sell them, and I'm trying to figure out when they'll be back." She hated lying, but in investigative journalism, you had to have a cover story ready.

"**LET ME CHECK** . . ." replied the receptionist, going over to her computer. "Here we are. It's been a few weeks since they occupied the **room**. Their last visit was a month ago."

"Thanks," Violet said.

Paulina and Violet sat down on a **SOFA** at the end of the hotel's lobby to discuss what they'd learned.

"If they were only here a month ago, the French couple couldn't have been the **thieves**," Paulina suggested. "Unless . . ."

"Unless they changed hotels to throw off

The Dupréses prepare for the opening of their new art gallery in London.

suspicion," concluded Violet *thoughtfully*.

The two mouselets didn't know what to do next. So Paulina started tapping at her MousePad. "Hey, look at this, Violet!" She showed her friend the screen.

Violet's eyes scanned the ARTICLE. "Hmm . . . the Dupréses have been in London for weeks preparing to open a new gallery," she read. "So they CAN'T be the thieves."

"*Exactly*," Paulina agreed. "Let's cross them off the list and start investigating our next suspect."

The two mouselets exchanged a **LOOK**.

"Countess Irina, here we come!" said Violet.

LET'S REVIEW THE SITUATION!

- The thefts at the mouseum have been occurring for two months, always on Thursday nights.
- The security system has never revealed anything unusual.
- There are five regular visitors to the mouseum, but Gavril's brother and the Duprés couple have strong alibis.
- Now Countess Irina and Andrej Goudanov are the chief suspects. Both have strong motives.

TRAGEDY AND NOBILITY

Paulina and Violet left the hotel and scurried toward COUNTESS IRINA'S mansion. The same butler who had welcomed them the night of the PARTY greeted them in the entryway.

"Whom may I announce to the countess?" he asked *formally*.

Hello! We know the countess . . .

"We met the countess at her *party*, and we'd LIKE to ask her a few questions about how she's descended from the Romanovs," Paulina began.

"That's right," Violet added quickly. "You see, we're students, and we want to *interview* her for our school newspaper."

"The countess is very *busy* —" the butler began, but a **shrill** squeak interrupted him.

"An article on how I descended from the *czars*? What a marvemouse idea!" the countess exclaimed. "Boris, make the mouselets comfortable in the blue room, and then bring us some TEA."

The butler led Violet and Paulina to a room decorated with elegant **BLUE** tapestries and motioned for them to have a seat.

"*Dearest mouselets*," the countess warbled, sinking onto a couch across from them. "I'm sure you would like to know all about **ME**! Very well . . . I will begin with my days as a mouseling in a luxurious mansion, where I lived with my family . . ."

The countess launched into the story of her life in some detail. Her tale was more boring than a cheese-free sandwich. The mouselets had to pinch their own tails to keep from falling asleep!

When the countess began to **describe** her noble origins, Paulina interrupted. "Are you really descended from the Romanovs? So you can trace your lineage back to the czars?"

Irina coughed. "Well, um . . . to be honest, no. And because of this minuscule detail, many don't believe me! Ah, these are such vulgar times, when rodents **doubt** the word of a noblemouse!"

The mouselets nodded, stifling giggles.

"I can only imagine how much you must ENJOY admiring the ancient family relics at the HERMITAGE," said Violet.

A smile spread across the countess's snout. "Ah, yes, they are magnificent! I just adore gazing at all that gold and those magnificent precious stones." Then she sighed. "And to think that those jewels should rightfully be mine!"

The mouselets exchanged a look.

"Do you go to the **MOUSEUM** often?" Violet asked. "Maybe you have a favorite day to visit . . . like Thursdays?"

"Oh no!" the countess exclaimed. "On Thursdays I have an APPOINTMENT I absolutely

never miss. You see, every Thursday evening Countess Sonia and Countess Diadora and I go out for an evening of **CULTURE** . . ."

Irina leaned in close as though she was about to let them in on a big secret. "We get together to **WATCH** our favorite television show, *Tragedy and Nobility*!" she whispered.

"**Ohhhhh** . . ." the mouselets murmured together.

This lead was a total dead end. The countess had the **perfect** alibi!

Oh, poor things!

There's no respect for the nobility!

ON THE TRAIL!

Meanwhile, Nicky and Gavril had their **SIGHTS** on Andrej Goudanov. The rodent had left the mouseum and scurried across the city streets. When he reached a spacious

SQUARE, he suddenly **STOPPED** and pulled out his cell phone.

"Who's he calling?" Nicky asked.

"Let's get closer," whispered Gavril, LEADING Nicky behind a bench.

"Are you ready?" the rodent said into his phone. "Yes, I have it . . . Okay, if you want . . ."

Just then a little mouse came up to Gavril and Nicky. "Are you playing hide-and-squeak?" he squeaked loudly.

"Shhhhh!" Nicky *hissed*. "Um . . . yes, we're hiding!"

The little mouse seemed convinced, and scampered away.

Nicky and Gavril kept listening to Goudanov's conversation, but they had missed a chunk of it because of the mouseling.

". . . give you the ring," he was saying.

Nicky and Gavril exchanged a look: the **RING**?! They were on the right track!

Suddenly, Goudanov ended his call and headed for the entrance to the **METRO**.

"Quick, let's follow him!" Gavril cried.

The metro station was CROWDED, and for a moment they lost sight of the collector.

"**There he is!**" Nicky suddenly cried. The two young mice *RUSHED* to buy tickets. Then they hurried after Goudanov.

They reached the platform just in time to

see him step into a car full of **passengers**.

Nicky and Gavril slid into the crowded subway car just before the doors closed. They were both *breathless*.

"Are you okay?" Gavril asked. Nicky

had turned as **PALE** as mold on Brie.

"I . . . I don't like being stuck in SMALL spaces . . ." she replied, looking around.

"Don't worry, we'll get off soon," Gavril reassured her, holding her paw **firmly**.

Nicky shot him a grateful smile. "This is turning out to be a pretty exciting chase!"

"That collector better look out, 'cause we're going to stick to him closer than a glue trap," the ratlet said. "He's getting off! Let's go!"

The rodents FOLLOWED the collector to the exit. For a moment, the SUN blinded them. Then they realized they were in front of **Moskovsky Station**, Saint Petersburg's main train depot. Goudanov was going inside, and the young rodents followed him.

Fifteen minutes later, they were climbing onboard a train to **Moscow**!

WE'VE GOT IT!
OR MAYBE NOT . . .

Four hours later, when Gavril and Nicky arrived in **MOSCOW**, the sun was already setting.

They HOPPED OFF the train just in time to see the collector climb into a *TAXI*. The two young rodents immediately stopped another one and CONTINUED the chase.

While Gavril kept his eyes on the **CAR** they were tailing, Nicky peered out her window at the **CITY** rushing by. She couldn't believe she was really in Moscow!

Just when they thought they'd be driving around the city forever, Goudanov's taxi stopped next to a large **SQUARE**.

"Let's get out, quick!" Gavril cried.

In the blink of a cat's eye, Nicky said good-bye to the taxi driver and started after Goudanov. Then an incredible **SIGHT** caught her attention.

"Ooooh! What's that?" she asked, pointing to a majestic building topped by colorful domes. It looked like something out of a fairy tale.

"SAINT BASIL'S CATHEDRAL," her friend explained. "Unfortunately, we don't have time to stop and check it out."

Saint Basil's Cathedral

Located in Red Square in Moscow, this historic cathedral was built between 1555 and 1561. Its unusual architecture, with turrets and curved, colorful domes, makes it one of the most distinctive buildings in all of Russia.

Goudanov was taking a side **STREET**. The rodents reached it in time to see him go into a **restaurant**. He sat down at a table where a ratlet was waiting for him.

"Let's go over there," Nicky whispered, pointing to a table from which they could easily keep an eye on him.

It looks like . . . a ring!

BORSCHT

This soup originally comes from Ukraine, but it is very common in Russia, too. The main ingredients are red beets, potatoes, and cabbage.

As the waiter brought them **soup**, the two mice talked quietly. After a few minutes, Goudanov took something out of his **jacket** pocket and gave it to the ratlet.

"It looks like a **ring** box!" Gavril whispered.

"Just as we **SUSPECTED**!" the mouselet cried, forgetting to be careful.

"Shhhhh." Gavril hushed Nicky as Goudanov got up and **HURRIED** toward the exit.

The young rodents were about to follow him when the waiter arrived to take their

ORDER. "What would you like?"

"um . . . actually, we . . ." Gavril began.

"May I suggest our world-famouse BORSCHT?"

Just then, the ratlet who had been seated with Goudanov **got up** and headed for the door.

"Thank you, but we just realized we're not hungry," Nicky said quickly. "Sorry, we have to *GO*!"

She took Gavril by the paw and scurried after the ratlet. They were finally about to get their paws on the **stolen ring!**

A SPECIAL RING

Outside the RESTAURANT, Nicky and Gavril looked around, feeling lost. What had happened to the rodent Goudanov was squeaking with?

"Over there! Don't let him ESCAPE!" said Nicky, pointing to a figure in the distance. They scampered after him. They'd almost reached him when . . .

"Aaahhhh!"

Gavril didn't notice the THIN layer of ice covering the sidewalk. He took a TUMBLE and slid right into the young rodent!

The ratlet was knocked to his paws, and the box he'd been carrying *flew* through the air. Nicky reached out and caught it before it hit the ground.

"S-sorry. Are you okay?" stuttered Gavril,

turning **pinker** than a cat's nose. He helped the ratlet get up.

"Yes, luckily everything's okay, but . . . Hey! That's mine!" the ratlet protested,

Let's go!

seeing his PRₑCĭoᴜs box in Nicky's paws.

"Actually, this belongs to the mouseum," she said confidently.

"Mŏuseụm?!" What mouseum?" the ratlet replied. "My father bought that at an **auction** in Omsk."

The ratlet took the box and opened it, revealing a ring with a flaming **RᴇD RᴜBY**. "It's beautiful, isn't it? So PRₑCĭoᴜs . . ."

Aaaahhhh!

Yiiiiiiikes!

"I'm sorry, there's been a misunderstanding," said Nicky. "We thought this was a **ring** stolen from the Hermitage. When we saw you meeting with that collector, we thought . . ."

The ratlet was *flabbergasted*. "That collector is my father! He bought the ring for me. I'm going to give it to a **special mouselet** with fur as red as this ruby!"

Nicky and Gavril exchanged a look. Their suspicions were more wrong than peanut butter on Gorgonzola!

Gavril apologized and said *good-bye* to the ratlet, but Nicky stopped him. "I have one last question. You said that your father bought the ring at an auction in Omsk . . . *Do you know when?*"

"Last Thursday. My father went back to Saint Petersburg on Friday, but he

The theft of the ring at the Hermitage happened last Thursday. All the suspects have alibis for that evening. Who else could have been at the mouseum?

couldn't come see me till today. Now you must excuse me. I can't wait to give this ring to my **SWEET** Anastasia!"

"So Goudanov has an alibi for the day of the **theft**," Nicky noted as the ratlet scurried away. She sent her friends a **text message** to update them.

The two mice returned to the station with their tails drooping in disappointment. They would have to take an overnight **train** to Saint Petersburg and continue their **INVESTIGATION** the next day.

Nicky:
Goudanov doesn't have the ring. We'll see you tomorrow morning at the mouseum.

Colette:
See you!

Nicky:
:)

An Ancient Secret

As her train sped through the night, Nicky called the other THEA SISTERS, and they filled her in on what they'd discovered.

Bright and early the next MORNING, Colette, Pam, Paulina, and Violet went to the steps of the Hermitage and waited there to meet Nicky and Gavril. "Our *investigation* is really at a dead end," Pam sighed.

Paulina nodded. They were all a little down in the snout.

"What's that?" Violet asked Colette, pointing to a **large** book sticking out of her friend's purse.

"I asked Aleksandra to lend me her **PHOTO** album. I want to show it to Gavril," Colette explained. "Maybe he can help us find another clue about the ring."

"Great IDEA! Let's give it another look right now," said Violet.

The friends started to flip through the album.

"Look at that **fabumouse** room," said Colette, admiring a photo of Yulia in an elegant drawing room. "It must be at the czar's court . . . which just happens to be the Palace we're standing in front of right now."

"Hey, I **recognize** that room!" said Paulina. "That's where Nicky and

Where has Paulina seen this room before?

I got LOST with Violet the other day. Doesn't it look familiar, Vi?"

"Yes, it sure does," Violet replied.

"Come on, then, let's go find it!"

Faster than the mouse who ran up the clock, Paulina began hurrying down the corridor. Her friends had no choice but to scurry after her.

"It was this way . . . No, that way . . ."

"Oh no, we're lost again!" Violet said.

"Nope — here we are!" her friend cried triumphantly.

The furniture was a little different, but there was no doubt: This was the same small but **splendid** room as in the photo.

"How **exciting**! This is Yulia's room," said Colette.

Paulina walked around the ROOM, inspecting it. "**SEE?** This is it! I recognized

it because of these decorations."

The mantelpiece was carved with different animal shapes: bears, deer, wolves, and an OWL.

Colette took the photo out of the ALBUM and held it up. "Look, it's still the same, and perfectly preserved!"

"Coco, what's written there?" asked Pamela curiously, pointing to something scrawled on the back of the photo.

"It's not writing," said Colette, turning over the PHOTO. "It's a drawing! Hmm . . . it looks like an owl."

Paulina studied the SKETCH, which was a bit faded by time. "Yes, but it's not just any owl . . . it's this owl!" She pointed to the carving above her.

"Well, it's not **exactly** the same as the drawing," Violet said. "See, this one has its

wings raised, while the one in the sketch has its wings **DOWN** . . ."

"Show me . . . You mean this wing?" Pam went up to the wall and pointed at the **carving**. But she got a bit too close, and her paw accidentally pressed down on the wing.

CLACK!

"Boiling borscht bites, I broke it!" the **mouselet** cried. "But how? I barely touched it!"

Her friends were about to **REPLY** . . . and then they realized Pam had set off a mechanism that opened up a **SECRET COMPARTMENT**!

"Look! There's something hidden in here," cried Colette, pulling out a notebook with a dark green cover.

The mouselets carefully flipped through the pages, which were yellowed by time.

"It looks like it might be —" Paulina began.

"A diary!" Colette finished. "YULIA'S diary, to be exact!"

YULIA'S DIARY

Colette brushed the *dust* off the cover and showed the diary to her friends. "Look, the name Yulia is written right here."

"**Great gouda!**" Pam exclaimed. "I can't believe we've uncovered a diary that belonged to Aleksandra's ancestor!"

Violet nodded. "This must have been her **SECRET** hiding place."

"So secret that the diary remained hidden all this time!" Violet concluded.

"Well, what are you waiting for, Colette? Let's **read it**!" Paulina said. "I'm practically crawling out of my fur with curiosity!"

The **mouseum** had just opened, and the rooms were still empty. So Colette opened the **diary**, whose yellowed pages were covered in a thin, *elegant* script, and began to read.

Dear diary,

Today something happened that has filled me with joy.

As I do every afternoon, I brought tea to my dear czarina. There was a ratlet showing her a beautiful necklace made of precious stones. I was about to place the tray on the table when he accidentally bumped into me. He apologized right away, and as he helped me dry the tray, our eyes met.

I immediately returned to my work, but his lively eyes and his shy, courteous manner left a deep impression on me.

I am a little shocked to be writing this! How can I be so preoccupied with someone I do not even know?

I must leave these questions unanswered. I am going to bed, for tomorrow I have a busy day awaiting me

"Cheese niblets! She must be talking about *Ivan*!" exclaimed Pam.

Colette *nodded*. "Uh-huh! Now we can hear the story from Yulia's point of view."

"Go on, Coco, keep reading!" Violet urged her. All the **FRIENDS** were impatient to hear more about this love story from LONG AGO.

Colette took a breath and continued.

Dear diary,
I was barely able to contain my excitement when I received a letter from an unknown address. The young rodent whom I saw with the czarina has written to me!

His name is Ivan, and he is the new court jeweler. He is making beautiful jewelry for the czarina. In his letter, he asked for my friendship . . .

He does not know that it is a useless request: My friendship, my affection, my thoughts have been his since the first moment I saw him.

"Love at first sight! It's just like Ivan put it in his letters!" Pam commented. "And then he and *Yulia* spent an afternoon **together**, right?"

"That's right," Colette replied, turning a few pages in the diary. "Okay, mouselets, scrape the cheese out of your ears and listen to this . . ."

Dear diary,
Today I had a truly unforgettable afternoon. Ivan came in his carriage to pick me up and take me for a trip. That ratlet surprised me, for he is not only kind and sweet, but also friendly and funny. The hours flew by as we laughed, joked, and talked.

When he drove me back home, he kissed my paw! I wished that moment would never end . . .

The mouselets all sighed at once. "What a **romantic** story! Keep **reading**!"

Dear diary,

Today I saw Ivan, as I have every Saturday for weeks now. This time we went for a trip along the Neva. Ivan said he wanted to bring me to a special place, but he didn't tell me anything about it until we reached a small field of fir trees covered in snow.

From there we could see the Neva, whose icy surface shone in the sunshine as a few mouselings skated across it.

He explained that his grandmother had often brought him there to play when he was little. I felt such tenderness for him as he talked about his past.

Before the others could **COMMENT**, Colette flipped a few pages ahead. "Mouselets, listen to what Yulia's diary says **next**!" she cried.

Dear diary,

I do not exaggerate when I say that today was the best day of my life!

Once again, Ivan brought me to the Neva, but I had no idea what he had planned! We sat together on a bench, and he took a small velvet bag out of his jacket and presented it to me. Then he waited anxiously as I opened it. Inside was a golden ring set with an exquisite alexandrite stone!

But it was his words that made my whiskers quiver, and I will never forget them: "My love, Yulia, I cannot imagine my future without you. I ask you to become my wife and to make me the happiest rodent in all of Russia."

Dear diary, my heart was overflowing with joy. I accepted him without hesitation!

"**AMAZING!**" Violet exclaimed.

"Yes," agreed Colette, wiping away a tear. "What a marvemouse love story . . ."

"No, not that!" Violet said. "Don't you see? We've finally solved the **MYSTERY** of the ring!"

What did Violet realize about the ring?

THE TWO RINGS

"Of course! Now I get it," Paulina said. "Ivan created two identical rings: one for the czarina, and the other for Yulia, the mouselet he *loved*!"

Colette closed the diary. "Aleksandra inherited the **ring** from her ancestor, while the czarina's was kept in the **mouseum** . . ."

"Until it was stolen!" Pam concluded. "WE'VE FINALLY SOLVED THE RIDDLE OF THE RING!"

"Riddle? So does that mean you mouselets are playing some kind of game?" a voice squeaked behind them.

It was Nicky and Gavril. Nicky sounded **grouchier** than a groundhog.

"We've been waiting for you at the entrance for half an hour! Did you forget we were supposed to **MEET**?"

"Sorry, Nic!" said Colette, throwing her arms around Nicky. "We've finally got a **SOLID** lead."

"And we've made an unbelievable discovery!" Violet added. Then she noticed that museum **VISITORS** were starting to file into the room. "Gavril, can we squeak in your **OFFICE**?"

We have news!

Oh?

The **mouselets** gathered around their friend's desk and told Nicky and Gavril about how they'd discovered the **DIARY**.

Then they described how they'd discovered that there were two **identical** rings!

"But . . . that's fabumouse!"

Nicky cried. "We can CLEAR Aleksandra's name."

"That's right. We just need to take Yulia's diary to the detective," Gavril put in. "So let's go give her the good news! She'll be happy to get back to training."

Violet sighed. "Yes, but we still haven't figured out the most important piece of the puzzle."

Paulina caught Gavril's CURIOUS look. "We still don't know who STOLE the czarina's ring," she explained.

"Did you and Nicky discover anything useful in Moscow?" Colette asked.

The ratlet shook his head. "Nope. Goudanov didn't have the RING we're looking for."

"In fact, he wasn't even in Saint Petersburg at the time of the theft," Nicky added.

The rodents were more confused

than a pack of cats in a dog kennel. They'd followed all the leads, but they were still no closer to solving the mystery! Who could the **THIEF** be?

LET'S REVIEW THE CLUES:

- Aleksandra's ring is identical to the one stolen from the Hermitage, but it's not the same one. Ivan the jeweler made two — one for the czarina, and one for Yulia.

- Yulia's diary proves the ring Aleksandra inherited isn't the one from the mouseum, which will clear Aleksandra's name.

- There's still one mystery to solve: Who stole the ring from the Hermitage? So far, all the suspects have alibis . . .

A SUSPECT ABOVE SUSPICION

The THEA SISTERS were glummer than a gerbil without a wheel. Now they could prove their friend's innocence, but they still had no *idea* who the real thief was.

"Who else could have committed the CRIME?" Nicky asked. "There aren't any other visitors who knew enough about the jewelry . . ."

"Gavril! There you are," Professor Rattensky exclaimed, bursting into the **office**. "I need your help to find — Oh! You mouselets are still here."

"Hello, PROFESSOR," Nicky said. "Gavril is helping us with our research."

Professor Rattensky stroked his WHISKERS. "Research . . . Artistic research? Historical research? I can't remember, my dear rodents."

"We're looking for the ring thief," Paulina explained.

The professor **NODDED**. "Of course. And have you found him?"

Gavril shook his snout. "We've followed a few different trails, but **NO** luck."

Leave it to the police!

"Oh, well, it's probably better to leave it to the **POLICE**, don't you think?" said the professor. "We academics must dedicate ourselves to what we do best: studying! **HEE, HEE, HEE!**"

As the professor chuckled, the mouselets exchanged a **LOOK**. Something about Professor Rattensky's behavior rubbed their fur the wrong way. He almost seemed happy their **investigation** had failed.

"Gavril, let's get back to work, OKAY?" said the professor.

The ratlet nodded. "Mouselets, Professor Rattensky is right — I really must get back to work. If you need anything else, you know where to **find** me."

Nicky sighed as Gavril followed the professor back into the galleries. "It's a shame we didn't uncover any more C L U E S."

"At least we've cleared Aleksandra," Colette replied. "Why don't we go let her know?"

The mouselets **HURRIED** out of Gavril's office and practically ran into Yuri, the security guard.

The professor is relieved the Thea Sisters and Gavril didn't discover anything ... but why?

"Oh, hello, Yuri," Nicky said.

"Hi, mouselets! How's your search going?"

"It's going nowhere," Pam *sighed*.

"I'm sorry to hear that. If anything **useful** comes to mind, I'll let you know," he assured them. "Now I've got to check the alarm system in Professor Rattensky's office. It's **messier** than a muskrat den in there!

Probably because the professor practically lives here."

"Okay, good luck . . ." Nicky began. Then she stopped. "Wait a minute. Did you say the professor spends a lot of time here?"

"Oh, tons of time! He's at the Hermitage more than any other rodent. It's for his research, you see. He has special permission to access all the Hermitage's most precious objects."

"And he comes to the mouseum every day?"

"Of course, Monday through Sunday, night and day. He's always here. Why do you ask?"

"Oh . . . just curious!" Nicky replied. "Excuse me, I need to go!" And she scurried down the corridor with the other THEA SISTERS on her tail.

"Moldy Brie on a baguette, you sure had a

lot of **QUESTIONS** for Yuri," Colette said as they left the mouseum.

"Because she *suspects* something!" replied Violet, who was already pawsteps ahead of her friends.

Nicky nodded. "Think about it: The professor moves freely around the mouseum. He's only been here for two months, and he arrived right around the time the **THEFTS** began. Every Thursday night he's alone because Gavril goes to play chess . . ."

"**WAIT, WAIT, WAIT!**" Colette cried. "Are you saying that . . ."

Violet nodded. "I think PROFESSOR RATTENSKY is our thief!"

> Professor Rattensky came to the Hermitage two months ago, just when the thefts began. Can it be a coincidence?

I DON'T BELIEVE IT!

Nicky decided not to follow her friends to Aleksandra's. Instead, she **RAN** back to warn Gavril. The ratlet was analyzing some artifacts and was surprised to **SEE** her again so soon.

"Nicky, what are you doing here?" he asked.

"I have to tell you something. Can we **STEP OUTSIDE** for a minute?"

"Well, actually, I have to work a while longer . . . I've already **lost** a lot of time to the investigation . . ."

"Please, it's very important. I promise it'll be quick!" Nicky pleaded.

Gavril noticed the **serious** expression on his friend's snout. After a moment of hesitation, he agreed.

They left the mouseum together and sat down on a **bench**.

"I don't know how to begin . . . Do you remember how we asked Yuri who visited the MOUSEUM the most over the past two months?" asked Nicky.

Gavril nodded. "Of course. That's where we began our search."

"That's right, but there's someone we've been forgetting since the BEGINNING, because he seemed to be above suspicion. I'm squeaking about someone who spends a lot of time at the **HERMITAGE**. Someone who's an expert on **jewelry**, who has the mouseum to himself every Thursday evening . . ."

Gavril frowned. "I don't understand. I can't think of anyone who fits that description."

"Think about it . . . It's someone you

KNOW well, because you work together," Nicky said gently.

"No! You can't be talking about Professor Rattensky?"

Nicky nodded. "He's our suspect. The clues fit **perfectly**!"

For a moment, Gavril stared **WIDE-EYED** at his friend. Then he burst out laughing.

Rattensky?

I'm afraid so . . .

"You're joking, right? How could you suspect the professor?"

"I know that it's **HARD** to believe, but please think about it. Everything matches up!"

Gavril **chewed** his whiskers. "I can't believe you're saying this. The professor is a **RESPECTED** academic who came here from abroad to conduct research on the **ROMANOV DYNASTY**. How can you think he's a criminal?!"

Nicky lowered her eyes. "I'm sorry, Gavril, but I **don't believe** we can exclude him from the list of suspects just because he works with you."

Gavril leaped to his paws. He was **madder**

I won't help you!

than a cat with a bad case of fleas. "It's not that! It's just that . . . I know him better than you do!"

"Gavril, don't you see? He's pulled the cheesecloth over your eyes!"

"Don't squeak! I don't want to hear it! If you want to include an innocent rodent in your INVESTIGATION, go ahead. But I won't help you do it!"

With that, Gavril turned and leaped up the STEPS to the mouseum.

Nicky stayed on the BENCH, alone, as big, icy snowflakes began to fall from the sky.

She couldn't believe how badly the conversation had gone.

A CLEVER TRAP

A little later, Nicky joined her friends at Aleksandra's HOUSE. When the skater heard her name had been cleared, her eyes filled with tears of joy.

To celebrate, Pavel prepared a **double batch** of blini. That made Pam happier than a hungry rat in a feta factory.

"I don't know what I would have done without you. You mice are worth your weight in **cheese**!" Aleksandra exclaimed, hugging the Thea Sisters.

Colette shrugged. "We got LUCKY!"

"Squeaking of luck," Paulina added, "we need to figure out how to PROVE our SUSPICIONS about Professor Rattensky."

"Maybe that's not a good idea," Nicky said. "I just squeaked with Gavril, and he's certain

the professor had nothing to do with it."

"Nicky, we can't **IGNORE** a good lead," Violet said. "This is hard for Gavril because he's close to the professor."

Pam nodded. "Sometimes you've gotta break a few eggs to make a cheesecake. The most **IMPORTANT** thing is uncovering the truth. If we're wrong, we'll find out!"

"You're right," Nicky admitted. "Where do we start?"

Colette had taken out her **PINK** notebook. "Why don't we set a trap?"

The friends exchanged a **LOOK**.

"A trap?"

"Yes. Listen . . ."

Half an hour later, the Thea Sisters were back on the steps of the **HERMITAGE**.

Colette scampered inside and

began looking for Professor Rattensky. She found him in a room full of paintings. He was studying the artwork and taking notes.

"Hello, professor. Still working?" she asked in a LOUD squeak.

The professor was startled. "Who . . . ? What . . . ? Do we know each other?"

"Yes, I'm a friend of Gavril's." Colette smiled. "You know, I'm investigating the theft of the ring."

"Oh, yes, of course!" the professor mumbled.

"Did you know that the investigation is finally at a turning point? The police have made a breakthrough!"

"A breakthrough?

There's been a breakthrough . . .

Really?

Really?" said the professor, suddenly interested.

"That's right. I hear they've found the loot: not just the ring, but the rest of the **STOLEN** jewelry, too. I'm sure they'll notify you soon."

The professor dropped his pen. "Really? What wonderful news! Do you know where they found it?"

Colette noticed his paws were trembling as he picked up his pen. "They didn't say. And I actually have to run. Bye!"

Colette hurried to rejoin the other mouselets **outside** the mouseum.

"The trap is set, sisters!" Colette whispered. "And from the way the professor's acting, I'd say he's guiltier than a gopher in a gerbil burrow."

They all crouched down together in a corner, keeping an eye on the exit. A few moments later, Rattensky **RUSHED** out and jumped into his car.

"Just as you **PREDICTED**, Coco. Let's follow him!" Nicky declared.

The **mouselets** hailed a taxi.

"Follow that car, but don't let it see us!" Pam told the **DRIVER**.

"What's going on, mouselets? Are you secret agents?" the driver asked, **laughing**.

"Kind of," Colette replied. "We're the Thea Sisters, and we're always chasing the **tRUtH**!"

Follow that car!

CAUGHT RED-PAWED!

After driving a few **miles**, Professor Rattensky stopped in front of a rundown **building**.

The Thea Sisters paid their fare and hopped out of their **TAXI** just in time to follow him through the front door.

"This place is creepier than Cacklefur Castle . . ." whispered Colette, giggling nervously.

The professor climbed up four flights in **DARKNESS** till he reached the door of an apartment. The Thea Sisters followed him on tiptoe.

"This is it!" Nicky murmured, her whiskers quivering.

The professor suddenly turned around, but in the **Dark** hallway he couldn't see anyone.

He took a heavy **KEY** out of his pocket and put it in the lock, which turned **noisily**. Then he went inside, closing the door behind him.

"Oh no! What do we do?" Paulina asked.

Colette crept up to the **door** and pushed it gently. "It's open!"

Quiet as mice, the Thea Sisters filed in. Rattensky was in the middle of the **ROOM**, his tail turned to them. He was fiddling with the dial on a large *safe*.

"Six . . . five . . . eighteen sixty-eight . . ." he muttered, entering the combination.

"That's the birthdate of the last czar!" Violet hissed.

"Ah, there you are. **My treasure!**" the professor said. "I knew that mouselet's story had more holes than a slice of Swiss."

"*Actually, you're the one whose story is full of holes!*" Nicky cried.

The professor **whipped** around. "Wh-what . . . ? Where did you come from?" he stuttered, trying to hide the open safe. The Thea Sisters could see it was filled with jewels and **glittering** gold objects.

"Gavril didn't believe us, but you really are the ***THIEF***!" Violet said.

"What are you saying? Me . . . no . . ."

"You can't deny it," Pam said.

"Maybe not. But I can keep you from **blabbing** about it, smartyfur!"

With that, Rattensky grabbed Nicky by the paw and rushed toward the mouselets. But Colette **TRIPPED** him, and he tumbled tail over snout.

"What a sorry end for such a distinguished professor!" Paulina **CRIED**.

"You said it, sis!" Pam agreed.

She'd just spotted some documents the professor had left on the table. "Why, look here, this says that your real name is actually **SIDNEY CROOKSON** . . ."

The phony professor got up, twisting his whiskers with frustration. Colette was ready to trip him again if he tried to **escape**. But it wasn't necessary.

"**I give up!**" the rodent cried. His snout

crumpled like a house of cheese crackers. "You're right . . . I'm not who I say I am. I'm a high-end art collector, specializing in the Romanov dynasty."

"Collector? More like thief!" Nicky cried. "But how did you pose as a professor?"

"Well, I'm a fine art expert . . . and I'm good at falsifying documents, and security footage, too."

"You fooled us all!" cried Pam.

Crookson sighed. "Couldn't we come to some kind of agreement and keep this between us? The police still don't know anything, right?"

"Actually, the POLICE know everything," Katerina's father declared. He'd just entered the apartment with two officers in tow.

"DETECTIVE, we've been expecting you!" exclaimed Paulina. She had texted the location of the phony professor's hideout to the police a few minutes earlier. "We've got the thief . . . and the **loot**!"

While the detective escorted Sidney Crookson to the police car, the Thea Sisters looked around with **satisfaction**. The truth had finally come to light, and the *case was closed!*

Mr. Crookson, follow me!

ALEKSANDRA'S
FiNAL TRIUMPH!

A few days later, the THEA SISTERS were on their way to the Ice Palace for the last round of the FIGURE-SKATING championship. Aleksandra and Pavel had received good scores in all their routines, qualifying them for the **finals**.

The mouselets were excited, but Nicky was a little **DOWN** in the snout.

"What's up, sis? Is that borscht not sitting well in your belly?" asked Pam, putting a paw around her **friend**.

Nicky's whiskers were drooping. "Nothing. It's just that, ever since we arrested that fake

Aleksandra:
Hi, mouselets, are you here?
I FEEL GREAT!

professor, I haven't heard anything from Gavril. *I wonder how he is . . ."*

"Well, why don't you ask him in the fur? Look over there!" Pam pointed to a **figure** heading toward them.

"Nicky, can I talk to you for a minute?" Gavril asked.

"Of course!" Nicky replied.

"Let's go inside. I want to get a good seat," Colette said, WINKING at her friends.

Nicky and Gavril were **ALONE** in front of the Palace.

"Nicky, I'm SORRY for the way I behaved the other day. I didn't believe your suspicions, but you were right," the ratlet began.

"Don't worry about it," Nicky said. "It must have been hard to learn the truth about the professor."

Gavril nodded. "It was. But I shouldn't have **pushed** you away like that. We've only known each other a few days, but I already consider you a TRUE friend." He took Nicky's paws in his and **SMILED**.

Nicky returned the **smile**. "Come on, the competition is about to begin!"

The two friends entered the Palace paw in paw.

The performances had already begun. Aleksandra and Pavel were among the last couples to COMPETE.

The mouselets held their breath as the pair made their entrance. They were wearing gorgeous COSTUMES decorated with crystals, and Aleksandra was positively **glowing**. Pavel was next to her, and beamed up at them. The skaters had six new friends CHEERING for them from the bleachers!

The music started, and the couple began to glide across the ice. Aleksandra's *graceful* movements MATCHED Pavel's perfectly.

The crowd was squeakless for the entire performance. At the end, the judges awarded Aleksandra and Pavel the highest score: They had won the championship! The Thea Sisters jumped up and down like mouselings after Santa Paws's visit.

Before Aleksandra could step onto the podium, Katerina approached her. "I wanted to **CONGRATULATE** you. You really deserved this win."

Aleksandra's snout fell open: Her rival was being NICE to her? Really?

"And . . . I wanted to tell you I'm sorry I pinned the theft on you," Katerina continued.

"You don't need to **apologize**. The

evidence was against me," Aleksandra replied.

"Do you think that . . . maybe . . . we could be **friends**?" Katerina asked.

Aleksandra smiled. "**OF COURSE!** On the ice, you'll always be my **RIVAL**. But that doesn't mean that we can't be friends!"

The Thea Sisters watched the scene with big smiles. At last Katerina recognized the value of true friendship . . . *just like they did every day*!

Don't miss these exciting Thea Sisters adventures!

Thea Stilton and the Dragon's Code

Thea Stilton and the Mountain of Fire

Thea Stilton and the Ghost of the Shipwreck

Thea Stilton and the Secret City

Thea Stilton and the Mystery in Paris

Thea Stilton and the Cherry Blossom Adventure

Thea Stilton and the Star Castaways

Thea Stilton: Big Trouble in the Big Apple

Thea Stilton and the Ice Treasure

Thea Stilton and the Secret of the Old Castle

Thea Stilton and the Blue Scarab Hunt

Thea Stilton and the Prince's Emerald

Thea Stilton and the Mystery on the Orient Express

Thea Stilton and the Dancing Shadows

Thea Stilton and the Legend of the Fire Flowers

Thea Stilton and the Spanish Dance Mission

Thea Stilton and the Journey to the Lion's Den

Thea Stilton and the Great Tulip Heist

Thea Stilton and the Chocolate Sabotage

Thea Stilton and the Missing Myth

Thea Stilton and the Lost Letters

Be sure to read all of our magical special edition adventures!

THE KINGDOM OF FANTASY

THE QUEST FOR PARADISE:
THE RETURN TO THE KINGDOM OF FANTASY

THE AMAZING VOYAGE:
THE THIRD ADVENTURE IN THE KINGDOM OF FANTASY

THE DRAGON PROPHECY:
THE FOURTH ADVENTURE IN THE KINGDOM OF FANTASY

THE VOLCANO OF FIRE:
THE FIFTH ADVENTURE IN THE KINGDOM OF FANTASY

THE SEARCH FOR TREASURE:
THE SIXTH ADVENTURE IN THE KINGDOM OF FANTASY

THE ENCHANTED CHARMS:
THE SEVENTH ADVENTURE IN THE KINGDOM OF FANTASY

THE PHOENIX OF DESTINY:
AN EPIC KINGDOM OF FANTASY ADVENTURE

THEA STILTON: THE JOURNEY TO ATLANTIS

THEA STILTON: THE SECRET OF THE FAIRIES

THEA STILTON: THE SECRET OF THE SNOW

THEA STILTON: THE CLOUD CASTLE

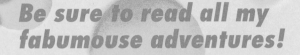

Be sure to read all my fabumouse adventures!

#1 Lost Treasure of the Emerald Eye

#2 The Curse of the Cheese Pyramid

#3 Cat and Mouse in a Haunted House

#4 I'm Too Fond of My Fur!

#5 Four Mice Deep in the Jungle

#6 Paws Off, Cheddarface!

#7 Red Pizzas for a Blue Count

#8 Attack of the Bandit Cats

#9 A Fabumouse Vacation for Geronimo

#10 All Because of a Cup of Coffee

#11 It's Halloween, You 'Fraidy Mouse!

#12 Merry Christmas, Geronimo!

#13 The Phantom of the Subway

#14 The Temple of the Ruby of Fire

#15 The Mona Mousa Code

#16 A Cheese-Colored Camper

#17 Watch Your Whiskers, Stilton!

#18 Shipwreck on the Pirate Islands

#19 My Name Is Stilton, Geronimo Stilton

#20 Surf's Up, Geronimo!

#21 The Wild, Wild West

#22 The Secret of Cacklefur Castle

A Christmas Tale

#23 Valentine's Day Disaster

#24 Field Trip to Niagara Falls

#25 The Search for Sunken Treasure

#26 The Mummy with No Name

#27 The Christmas Toy Factory

#28 Wedding Crasher

#29 Down and Out Down Under

#30 The Mouse Island Marathon

#31 The Mysterious Cheese Thief

Christmas Catastrophe

#32 Valley of the Giant Skeletons

#33 Geronimo and the Gold Medal Mystery

#34 Geronimo Stilton, Secret Agent

#35 A Very Merry Christmas

#36 Geronimo's Valentine

#37 The Race Across America

#38 A Fabumouse School Adventure

#39 Singing Sensation

#40 The Karate Mouse

#41 Mighty Mount Kilimanjaro

#42 The Peculiar Pumpkin Thief

#43 I'm Not a Supermouse!

#44 The Giant Diamond Robbery

#45 Save the White Whale!

#46 The Haunted Castle

#47 Run for the Hills, Geronimo!

#48 The Mystery in Venice

#49 The Way of the Samurai

#50 This Hotel Is Haunted!

#51 The Enormouse Pearl Heist

#52 Mouse in Space!

#53 Rumble in the Jungle

#54 Get into Gear, Stilton!

#55 The Golden Statue Plot

#56 Flight of the Red Bandit

The Hunt for the Golden Book

#57 The Stinky Cheese Vacation

#58 The Super Chef Contest

#59 Welcome to Moldy Manor

The Hunt for the Curious Cheese

#60 The Treasure of Easter Island

#61 Mouse House Hunter

Don't miss my journeys through time!

Meet
GERONIMO STILTONOOT

He is a cavemouse — Geronimo Stilton's ancient ancestor! He runs the stone newspaper in the prehistoric village of Old Mouse City. From dealing with dinosaurs to dodging meteorites, his life in the Stone Age is full of adventure!

#1 The Stone of Fire

#2 Watch Your Tail!

#3 Help, I'm in Hot Lava!

#4 The Fast and the Frozen

#5 The Great Mouse Race

#6 Don't Wake the Dinosaur!

#7 I'm a Scaredy-Mouse!

#8 Surfing for Secrets

#9 Get the Scoop, Geronimo!

MEET
GERONIMO STILTONIX

He is a spacemouse — the Geronimo Stilton of a parallel universe! He is captain of the spaceship *MouseStar 1*. While flying through the cosmos, he visits distant planets and meets crazy aliens. His adventures are out of this world!

#1 Alien Escape

#2 You're Mine, Captain!

#3 Ice Planet Adventure

#4 The Galactic Goal

#5 Rescue Rebellion

Meet
CREEPELLA VON CACKLEFUR

Geronimo Stilton, have a lot of mouse fiends, but none as **spooky** as my friend CREEPELLA VON CACKLEFUR! She is an enchanting and MYSTERIOUS mouse with a pet bat named **Bitewing**. YIKES! I'm a real 'fraidy mouse, but even I think CREEPELLA and her family are AWFULLY fascinating. I can't wait for you to read all about CREEPELLA in these a-mouse-ly funny and **spectacularly spooky** tales!

#1 The Thirteen Ghosts

#2 Meet Me in Horrorwood

#3 Ghost Pirate Treasure

#4 Return of the Vampire

#5 Fright Night

#6 Ride for Your Life!

#7 A Suitcase Full of Ghosts

THANKS FOR READING,
AND GOOD-BYE UNTIL OUR
NEXT ADVENTURE!

TheaSisters